GEOFF SWIFT
Tommy the Fieldmouse's
Night-Time Adventures

©2022 by Geoff Swift

Design and Illustration by Jane Cornwell
www.janecornwell.co.uk
Jane's Studio Press

ISBN: 978-1-7398281-5-8

For Jane,
who has illustrated all of my books,
Geoff.

For Geoff,
thank you for your support and encouragement,
and for my son Grant,
who looks after the wildlife in our garden.

Jane

Grain Crop Facts

Around the World, grains, also called cereals, are the most important staple food for humans and some animal species.

Grains are a good source of, fibre, carbohydrates, protein, and a wide range of vitamins and minerals.

Field Mouse on Rye Grain

Field Mouse and Rice Plant

Grain is grown on over 17 percent of the total cultivated land in the world

Humans get an average of 48 percent of their calories or food energy, from grains.

5

Field Mouse and Buck Wheat

Field Mouse and
Barley Grain

There are many types
and variations of grain
including: wheat, rye,
barley, millet, corn, rice,
quinoa, buckwheat, and
many more.

Field Mouse and
Millet Grain

How many more do you
think?

Can you think of any
human food made with
grain?

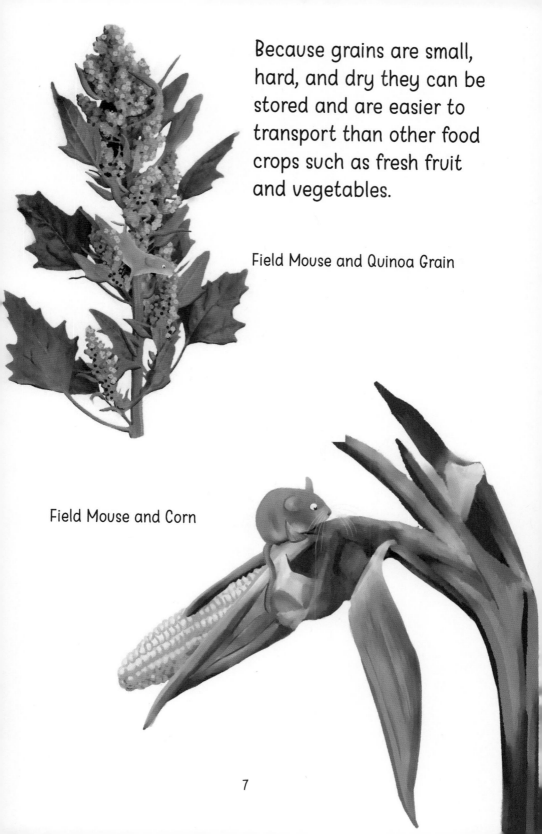

Because grains are small, hard, and dry they can be stored and are easier to transport than other food crops such as fresh fruit and vegetables.

Field Mouse and Quinoa Grain

Field Mouse and Corn

Chapter One

Tommy slowly turned over and stretched out his body and tail. He opened his eyes, yawned, and looked around the gloom in the burrow. His friend, Max the Rabbit, was still sleeping, so Tommy slowly crawled away, not to disturb him. He headed to one of the entrances to the burrow he shared with Max. Tommy's tummy rumbled, he was hungry and needed to search for his supper.

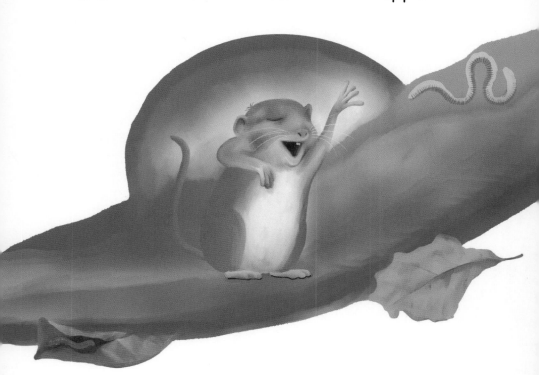

Earlier that day Max had saved Tommy from Hissing Sid, the poisonous adder who had been about to strike Tommy. Hissing Sid was just one of the many creatures Tommy had to look out for. There were lots of creatures who would love to catch Tommy and his friend Max and eat them. So, every day was a fight for survival.

Tommy looked out from the burrow his whiskers twitching as he sniffed the air.

It was a calm windless summer evening which would help Tommy hear any predators as he searched for his supper.

Tommy knew where to get a scrumptious tasty meal, on the other side of the river. The farmer had a crop of wheat with juicy seeds, which was almost ready to harvest. Being on the other side of the river wasn't going to stop Tommy from reaching it. There were two ways to cross. There was a large gas pipeline which lots of creatures used, a bit like the humans' main road, but that was too busy and risky.

Tommy preferred the other way,
across the river by ferry.

Chapter Two

Tommy headed to the riverbank looking for the ferry. He scampered up and down the bank until he saw the ferry across the other side of the river. He whistled, shouted, jumped up and down until he got the ferry's attention.

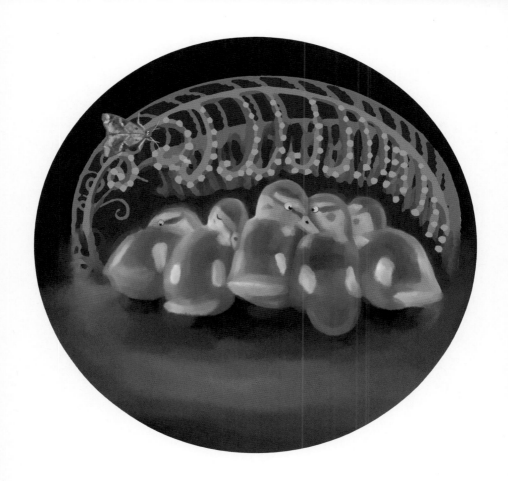

Beth the Duck looked across, saw Tommy, and
waved a wing in acknowledgment. Bobbing beside
her were her five ducklings. Beth spoke to the
ducklings, who formed into a flotilla, then paddled
off to an overhanging shrub on the bank to hide.
When Beth was sure the ducklings were safely
hidden, she paddled across the river to Tommy.

'Hi Tommy' she quacked, 'I suppose you want a lift across the river.'

Tommy smiled 'You're the best ferry service on the river, can I hitch a ride to the other side? Please!'

Beth smiled, turned, and slowly backed onto the bank lowered her tail, and shouted, 'All aboard! This ferry is leaving for the other side of the river.'

Tommy laughed, ran down the bank and up Beth's tail onto her back. When Beth felt Tommy sit on her back, she pushed off across the fast-flowing river.

As she paddled, she lowered her head onto her back and said to Tommy, 'Climb up on my head, so we can talk without me turning round to face you.' Tommy climbed up and stretched out on Beth's head. When Beth felt Tommy settle, she raised her head with Tommy on top, and continued paddling, then asked Tommy where he was going.

Tommy explained he was going to the wheat field to get his supper. As they neared the bank Beth's ducklings swam out, towards their mum.

When the ducklings saw Tommy sitting on their mum's head, they all burst out laughing.

They were laughing so much they started beating their wings up and down on the water. Their beating created waves that made Beth bob up and down forcing Tommy to hold on tight.

'Stop it!' Beth shouted at her ducklings, 'Your waves are making Tommy hold on so tight, he's nipping my head, so he doesn't fall off. Stop it!'

By this time, the ducklings were alongside their mum. 'Hi Tommy!' they shouted in unison.

'Hi' Tommy shouted back.

Steph, one of the ducklings, shouted to Tommy 'You've no idea how funny you look on top of mum's head. Where are you going?'

'I'm going to the wheat field to get my supper.' Tommy replied,' I fancy some wheat grains and the crop is ready to eat. I know it must look funny, but I am so small and only have a small squeaky voice, it would be hard to talk to your mum from her back. Anyway, here we are at the shore, I'll see you all later, take care.'

When they reached the shore Beth angled her beak onto the bank so Tommy could run down from her head, up her beak, and onto the bank.

Tommy shouted his thanks as he ran into the undergrowth to hide from predators. He waited a few minutes, sniffed the air, twitched his whiskers, looked around, and listened. He wanted to make sure it was safe to go to the wheat field.

When Tommy was happy it was safe, he ran through the undergrowth using trails other small mammals had previously used. These trails were created and made over many years to provide safe routes and refuges for all the small creatures.

Chapter Three

Tommy reached the edge of the wheat field. By this time, he was very hungry, but he knew from experience to wait, look, and listen before going into the field. When Tommy was sure it was safe, he scampered off.

Looking up he saw a wheat sheaf with ripe seeds. This was the stalk for him. He was so light the sheaf hardly moved as he climbed up it. He reached the head then started eating the seeds. To Tommy, this was a feast.

Tommy was munching his way through the seeds when he sensed a threat. He dropped the seed he was eating and fell like a stone to the ground, twisting and turning in mid-air so he would land on his feet. As he dropped, he heard a WHOOSH behind him and the sheaves above move, raining wheat seeds down on top of him.

Tommy didn't stop. He ran as fast as he could to a small overhanging rock. Tommy reached the rock and backed himself in as far as he could, turned, then slowly peered around outside. There was no threat on the ground, so he looked at the sky, then the trees. Still nothing...

Tommy stayed still, as he looked, he could hear
his heart beating in his ears. There was something
out there and it had seen Tommy. After minutes
of looking around Tommy saw a movement up in a
tree. Tommy focused on the tree, then a branch.

Oh No! Tommy's worst nightmare!
Grant the Barn Owl was looking straight at him.

Grant rotated his head almost fully around,
then turned back to stare at Tommy with big
unblinking eyes.

Tommy backed further into the rock. He was
trapped. The minute he left the safety of the rock,
Grant would silently swoop down, then strike with
his sharp claws, and carry him off. Tommy looked
from side to side then sat down to wait, he was no
longer hungry but trapped under the rock.

After twenty minutes Tommy heard a 'Twit Twoo, Twit Twoo,' across the other side of the field. Tommy thought, 'Oh No! Another owl!'

Tommy slowly stuck his head out to look. As he watched he heard a distant 'Twoo, Twit Twoo' again.

This time, however, Grant replied 'Twit Hwoo, Hwoo,' then flew off towards the other side of the field and to the other owl.

Chapter Four

Tommy didn't hang around, he had to make his escape now. There was only one way to get back over the river, the gas pipeline. Beth and the ducklings would be asleep in a safe shelter on the riverbank. The pipeline was the only option.

Tommy ran as fast as his little legs would carry him then reached the pipeline. He hid in the undergrowth to catch his breath and to see if it was safe to cross.

After several minutes, he decided to move. He had one last look around, checked the sky then ran onto the pipeline. He was over halfway across when he saw a movement ahead. Slowly walking onto the pipeline from the other side, was Jane the fox.

Tommy skidded to a halt. He was in big trouble. He was over halfway across. If he turned and ran Jane would catch him before he reached the bank. He looked at the water, it was too fast, deep, and cold for Tommy to swim.

Jane was slowly walking along the pipeline, her bushy brown tail swishing from side to side. She was closing the gap on Tommy. Her white fangs were glistening in the moonlight. Tommy looked around still trying to work out an escape route when something caught his eye.

Tommy slowly walked towards Jane. Her grin just got bigger and bigger. Tommy was trapped.

Suddenly, Tommy ran as fast as he could towards Jane. She couldn't believe her luck, the stupid mouse thought HE could attack HER! She would just gobble him up when he reached her then he would be finished, no more Tommy. Tommy ran as fast as he could to reach Jane.

Just as she pounced, Tommy slid between her claws as a dark cloud passed over them.

WHOOSH! Great big talons reached down and knocked Jane into the river!

Tommy ran as fast as he could, reaching the river bank safely.

Chapter Five

When Tommy reached the shelter of the undergrowth he turned and looked back at the river. He could see Jane paddling furiously with her bushy tail floating on the water behind her heading for the far bank.

Tommy calmed down, took a deep breath, then ran down the narrow track. He ran around a blind bend at full speed into a black and white hairy object. Tommy went flying, cartwheeling through the air, his tail whipping around before he landed with a bump.

'Who's there!?' Susie the badger shouted.

'Only me, Tommy.' Tommy replied.

'Didn't you see me, are you blind? I thought it only badgers that are short-sighted.' Susie asked.

'I'm sorry,' Tommy replied,' 'I've had a scary night. I've been chased by Grant the owl and Jane the fox, I just want to get safely home to my burrow and get to sleep.'

'Well, why are you hanging around here chatting to me? You better get going just in case Grant and Jane are still looking for you. Bye.'

And with that Susie ambled off, nose to the ground in search of fat juicy worms for her supper.

After the night's adventures, there was only one thing on Tommy's mind, a safe burrow, and a good night's sleep. He scampered off heading for home and his warm, snuggly bed. There would be more adventures looking for food, he had no doubt. But those would be for tomorrow night.

A few facts about the main characters.

Tommy - Like all mice Tommy is nocturnal, meaning he likes to sleep during the day and come out at night. He likes to eat fruits, seeds, and grains but if hungry will eat anything including electric cables (Uck).

Mice are clever and can solve many problems which helps them survive. If caught by a predator, they can shed their tails. Mice are very good jumpers and can jump up to eighteen inches. Tommy is also a very good climber and swimmer (but not in fast icy water).

Beth — Ducks like Beth can see underwater, and eat grain, seeds, nuts, fruit, insects, and small fish. They have webbed feet which allow them to paddle on the water. Duck feet have no nerves or blood vessels, which means their feet don't feel the cold. All ducks float on waterproof feathers. Their feathers interlock and are waxed which keeps them warm and dry.

Grant - Owls can live up to twenty-five years. A group of owls is called a Parliament.

Owls, like mice, are nocturnal and usually hunt at night. Owls very rarely drink water to hydrate. They get most of the hydration (fluids) they need from the prey they feast on.

Their vertebrae (backbone) have double the amount, of small bones, compared to normal birds. This allows them to turn their heads to an astonishing TWO HUNDRED and SEVENTY DEGREES! (Wow)

Jane - Foxes are one of the most adaptable creatures in nature. They live and adapt to their location, country, town, or city.

They are scavengers and can eat most things, even jam sandwiches. Foxes can run up to thirty miles per hour, making them able to run down their prey. A fox's tail makes up a third of its body length. When a fox grins (showing its teeth), it is afraid.

Susie - Badgers are nocturnal and active at night.
They have black and white faces and a short grey
body with black and white areas underneath.
They have very sharp hooked claws for digging,
but if threatened, will use them to fight.

They are clean animals living in shared burrows.
They leave their burrows when they need
the toilet. They can eat up to seven hundred
earthworms a night! However, they will also eat
fruits and other small insects they find.

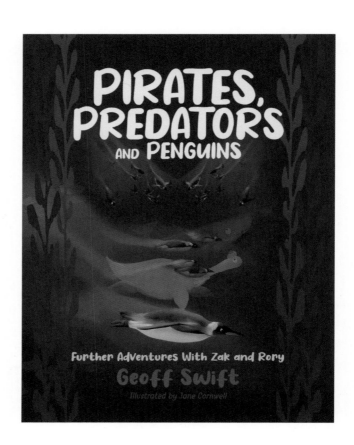

PIRATES, PREDATORS AND PENGUINS

Further Adventures With Zak and Rory

Geoff Swift

Illustrated by Jane Cornwell

GEOFF SWIFT
Max the Rabbit's
CLOSE ENCOUNTERS

GEOFF SWIFT
Brian The Beetroot's
Haircut

More stories by Geoff Swift

The Friendly Giant Called Zak and his Friend
Rory the Misnamed Monster

Rory Never Learns:
A Mediterranean Sea Adventure With Zak and
Rory

Zak and Rory's Toughest Journey:
With Zak and Rory

Pirates, Predators and Penguins,
Further Adventures With Zak and Rory

The Witch, The Cat and Jack:
A Trilogy of Witch stories and drawings

Brian the Beetroot's Haircut

Max the Rabbit's Close Encounters

About Geoff Swift

Geoff is the author of 'The Zak and Rory' series of books and 'The Witch, The Cat and Jack' Trilogy. He continues researching for The Zak and Rory series, and is enjoying the shared journey with the characters. He has also enjoyed working with Jane Cornwell the Scottish artist and illustrator, who has supported Geoff with the artwork and illustrations in all his books.

Geoff enjoys the outdoors and travelling, is a keen walker, skier and golfer when not writing. Geoff has given primary school talks, loves the engagement, feedback and questions the young learners give. Listening and engaging with the young learners, Geoff is impressed with their approach to learning and the environment.

As the future of the world is in their hands, the future looks good.

Twitter. @swift_geoff
www.geoffswiftwriter.com

Printed in Great Britain
by Amazon

28749114R00030

Tommy the Fieldmouse's Night-Time Adventures is a charming story for young readers by Geoff Swift.

'I'm going to the wheat field to get my supper. I fancy some wheat grains and the crop is ready to eat.'

When Tommy wakes up very hungry, the little fieldmouse is determined to make his way to the wheat field for some tasty grains. However, he encounters many dangerous predators on the way. Maybe, just maybe, with the help of his friends, Tommy will make his way safely home.

An exciting adventure in independent reading for young naturalists.

ISBN 9781739828158

9 781739 828158

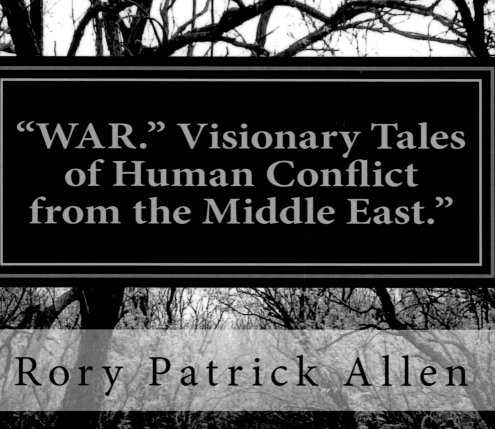

"WAR." Visionary Tales of Human Conflict from the Middle East."

Rory Patrick Allen